LATINOS IN BASEBALL

Ivan Rodriguez

Tony DeMarco

Mitchell Lane Publishers, Inc.
P.O. Box 200
Childs, MD 21916-0200

LATINOS IN BASEBALL

Tino Martinez	Bobby Bonilla	Roberto Alomar	Pedro Martinez
Moises Alou	Sammy Sosa	**Ivan Rodriguez**	Bernie Williams
Ramon Martinez	Alex Rodriguez	Vinny Castilla	Manny Ramirez

First Printing

Library of Congress Cataloging-in-Publication Data

DeMarco, Tony (Anthony P.)
     Ivan Rodriguez / Tony DeMarco.
        p. cm. — (Latinos in baseball)
     Summary: A biography of the catcher for the Texas Rangers, Ivan Rodriguez, who made his major league debut at age nineteen.
     ISBN 1-58415-006-8
     1. Rodriguez, Ivan, 1971—Juvenile literature. 2. Baseball players—Puerto Rico—Biography—Juvenile literature. [1. Rodriguez, Ivan, 1971- 2. Baseball players. 3. Puerto Ricans—Biography.] I. Title. II. Series.

GV865.R623 D46 2000
796.357'092—dc21
[B]
                                    99-053058

About the Author: Tony DeMarco is a freelance writer who has covered major-league baseball since 1985 for the *Denver Post*, *MSNBC Online*, the *Fort Worth Star Telegram*, and the *Miami Herald*. He has also authored biographies of Vinny Castilla, Larry Walker, and Ed McCaffrey. His articles have appeared in *The Sporting News*, *Sport Magazine*, *Beckett's Baseball*, *The Complete Handbook of Baseball*, and *Peterson's Baseball*. He lives in Englewood, Colorado.

Photo Credits cover: Otto Greule/Allsport; pp. 4, 6, 7 Otto Greule/Allsport; p. 23 Joe Patronite/Allsport; pp. 26, 30, 35, 40 © Corbis; p. 46, 51, 52 Otto Greule/Allsport; p. 49 David Seelig/Allsport; p. 53 Craig Melvin/Allsport

Acknowledgments: The following story was developed based on the author's personal interviews with Ivan Rodriguez on June 13 and July 26, 1999. Professional and personal friends and family members were also interviewed for this book, including: Luis Mayoral (June 13, July 26, and August 30, 1999), Bobby Valentine (May 12, 1999), Rafael Palmeiro (June 10, 1999), Juan Gonzalez (June 10, 1999), and Tom Grieve (June 11, 1999). This story has been thoroughly researched and checked for accuracy. To the best of our knowledge, it represents a true story. The author and publisher gratefully acknowledge the cooperation and helpfulness of Ivan Rodriguez in the development of this book.

Mitchell Lane PUBLISHERS

JAN - - 2001

TABLE OF CONTENTS

At the young age of 28, Ivan is already an eight-time All-Star.

CHAPTER ONE
The Big Day

From a justice of the peace's office in Tulsa, Oklahoma, to Comiskey Park in Chicago, June 20, 1991, was the biggest day in Ivan Rodriguez's young life.

Ivan, all of 19 years old, married Maribel Rivera in the morning and made his major-league debut that evening. Topping it off, he singled in two runs in the ninth inning to cap a 7-3 Texas Rangers' victory.

If it didn't happen, you would think it was the script from a made-for-TV movie. It was too good to be true. But the fact is, it wasn't supposed to happen quite the way it did.

The plan had been for Ivan and Maribel, who met three years earlier in Puerto Rico, to be married on the field at Tulsa's Drillers Stadium between games of a double-header on the night of June 20. But the Texas Rangers had other ideas. Their catching situation had been troublesome all season, with teams able to steal bases against them almost at will. Meanwhile, Ivan—already marked as the team's catcher of the future—was proving to be too good for Double-A Texas League competition.

Two weeks earlier, the Rangers had considered calling Ivan up to the major leagues, but he had an injured hand at the time. But when Geno Petralli, one of the Rangers' three catchers, suffered a lower-back injury that forced him onto the disabled list, the Rangers could wait no longer. Wedding ceremony or not, Ivan's time had come.

The decision was made on the night of June 19, and Rangers general manager Tom Grieve placed a phone call to Tulsa manager Bobby Jones. Ivan was to be in the Drillers' starting lineup that night as the catcher. But as a precaution, Grieve had Jones switch Ivan to the designated-hitter spot. Grieve also gave Ivan the option of staying in Tulsa for the wedding ceremony scheduled for the following night. But Ivan was so anxious to get to the major leagues, he decided otherwise without telling Maribel.

Ivan's powerful throwing arm is widely regarded as the best in the major leagues.

"Going to the big leagues is what I've been wanting to do all my life," Ivan said that day.

A disappointed Maribel said, "I have no idea what we're going to do. I sort of had a feeling this would happen."

What they did was visit the county courthouse in the morning, get married in a civil ceremony, then board a flight to Chicago. Who needed a wedding reception when the big leagues were waiting? Besides, there would be more to celebrate after the game.

Although he was the youngest player in the major leagues when he made his debut, and would

Ivan has won eight consecutive Gold Glove Awards on the strength of his throwing arm and cat-quick reactions behind home plate.

continue to hold that designation all the way through the 1991 and 1992 seasons, Ivan made an auspicious debut.

It didn't take long for the White Sox to find out about Ivan's powerful right arm, as he threw out both Warren Newson and Joey Cora attempting to steal. And at the plate, where he was expected to struggle, Ivan got a key two-run single off Melido Perez to go 1 for 4.

"It was a crazy day, in a positive way," Ivan said. "Getting married was wonderful, and I got a hit in the game. But throwing out two guys, that made the day unforgettable. I really felt proud."

Tom Grieve has another memory of the night.

"I'll never forget it," Grieve said. "Pudge [Ivan] walked out to the mound because our pitcher [Kevin Brown] was throwing over to first base, all concerned about the runner. You could see him make the motion that was saying, 'Throw the ball to me. I'll take care of the rest. Don't worry about the runner.' I also remember that he threw the runner out by about 30 feet. It was unbelievable. He was 19, in his first game."

And the best was yet to come.

CHAPTER TWO
The Gifted One

Right from the beginning, it was obvious. Ivan Rodriguez had been given a special gift.

As early as Little League baseball in Vega Baja, Puerto Rico, the short, squatty kid who would be tagged with the nickname "Pudge" later in life, could throw a baseball like nobody else. He was a pitcher back then, simply because he threw the ball so hard. The seven no-hitters he pitched in Little League came with only one pitch—a fastball. He didn't need anything else.

"Everybody was afraid to face me," Ivan said. "They were afraid I was going to hit them. Nobody could hit my fastball."

Ask anybody about the first time they saw Ivan—whether it was back in his youth baseball days, in the minor leagues or in the majors—and they say the same thing. They express amazement at how hard and accurately he can throw.

For Juan Gonzalez, who also grew up in Vega Baja and has played on the Texas Rangers with Ivan since 1991, that first meeting came on a playing field in their hometown.

"He always had a strong arm," Gonzalez said. "Right away, you could see that. He was small, but he could throw. I'm not surprised at how good he is now."

For Luis Mayoral, a Puerto Rican general manager, broadcaster and journalist who works for the Texas Rangers in an advisory capacity to the team's Latin players, that first meeting came 12 years ago before a Puerto Rican winter league game.

"Ivan was playing catch in the bullpen," Mayoral recalled. "I took one look at him and said to myself, 'What is this? My God, this kid was given a gift.' He was abnormal even then. When a guy is that good, it's unthinkable. In Spanish, we would say, *un aborto de la naturaleza*—an abortion of nature."

For Orlando Gomez, a former Rangers coach who now is coaching with the Tampa Bay Devil Rays, the first meeting was at a tryout camp in Puerto Rico that led to the Rangers signing Ivan at age 16.

"His arm was incredible," Gomez said. "He threw the ball all over the place, but the velocity and arm strength were there. There was no doubt about it. You knew Pudge was special."

Ivan, who has no middle name, was born November 30, 1971, in Vega Baja, the second son of Jose Rodriguez and Eva Torres. His older brother, Jose, Jr., two years Ivan's senior, played at the top level of amateur baseball in Puerto Rico, but never was signed by a major-league team. Ivan's father also was a top amateur baseball player, and was the biggest influence on Ivan's early development in the game. It was Ivan's father who strongly urged Ivan to begin catching in Little League, as he knew Ivan wouldn't grow to be very tall, and that few major-league pitchers are under six feet tall. The two would practice together a few times a week after Jose, Sr. finished with his work as an electrical supervisor for the Fluor Daniel Construction Company.

"He was the one who always helped me the most," Ivan said.

Soon after Ivan began catching, he became a fan of Johnny Bench of the Cincinnati Reds, widely regarded as the best catcher ever to play in the majors, as well as Lance Parrish of the Detroit Tigers, a perennial All-Star in the 1980s.

Ivan's parents divorced when he was 12, but he remained close to both before he signed professionally, and is still close to them today. His mother teaches second grade at Padilla Elementary School in Vega Baja, and his father still lives in the same house where Ivan and Jose Jr. were raised. Ivan returns each winter to Puerto Rico, and now lives only about one-half hour from Vega Baja, in a suburb of San Juan, the island's biggest city.

The neighborhood, or barrio, where Ivan grew up is known as Algarrobo. It sits on the outskirts of Vega Baja, a city of about 60,000 people located 18 miles west of San Juan, the island's biggest city, and about five miles south of the Atlantic Ocean. The area is part of a valley of mostly open pastureland, some of which used to be sugarcane plantations, and is about one-quarter mile east of the Cordillera mountain range that bisects Puerto Rico.

Ivan was a quiet and shy youngster, but displayed a love for baseball very early. A Little League All-Star team, which also included Gonzalez, made it all the way to the Puerto Rican championship series. Little did Ivan and Gonzalez know at the time that they would play together again years later in the major leagues. By the time Ivan was 15 and playing in the area Mickey Mantle League, his arm made him a major-league prospect despite the fact he would grow to be only five feet nine inches tall.

One scout in particular kept a little closer eye on Ivan than the others—Luis Rosa of the Rangers. Rosa already had scoured the island for years, signing future major-league stars such as Benito Santiago, Roberto and Sandy Alomar, Carlos Baerga, Jose Guzman, and Wilson Alvarez, as well as Gonzalez, who is two years older than Ivan.

Rosa was the manager of Ivan's Mickey Mantle League team, and to keep Ivan from being spotted by scouts from other teams, he would try to play Ivan only when they weren't around. At that point, Puerto Rican natives weren't subject to Major League Baseball's amateur draft, which gives every team a chance to select a player. If Rosa or another scout wanted to sign a player to a contract, they could do so on the spot. In the case of Gonzalez, a big and strong slugger, he received $140,000 from Rosa and the Rangers because several other teams made bids for him.

When Ivan was 16, he attended a July tryout camp arranged by Rosa for the Rangers, who sent scouting director Sandy Johnson and top scout Doug Gassaway, as well as Orlando Gomez. Rosa was touting some of his other players to be signed, but when Gassaway timed one of Ivan's throws to second base at a major-league-caliber 88 m.p.h., the attention turned to Ivan.

"At a tryout camp, a short, stocky kid isn't going to stand out by what he looks like," Grieve said. "It was his arm. Sandy told Luis to sign Ivan immediately, and we'll talk about the other guys later. He made sure Ivan was priority number one to get signed."

For a bargain-basement price of $15,000, a deal was struck, and Ivan was on his way to becoming one of the greatest catchers ever to play the game.

CHAPTER THREE
A Quick Climb

When it came time for Ivan's first pro season, the plan was to bring him to spring training, then let him stay in the extended minor-league spring-training program until the rookie league season began in June. But it was Orlando Gomez who suggested another plan. Gomez, who managed the Rangers' Class A farm team in Gastonia, North Carolina, that season, wanted to bring Ivan with him for a full season that began in April.

Bypassing the rookie league for the tougher Class A level would be a big step for a 17-year-old who barely spoke English, but Gomez promised to keep an eye on Ivan both on and off the field, and the Rangers agreed to send Ivan there.

"I had to fight for him," Gomez said. "They weren't going to send him there. He was real young. But the God-given ability was there. I thought he was a special kid who you could push to another level. And he ended up having a good year. I was only going to catch him three or four times a week. But the way he was going, he caught almost every game. He handled the pitchers great, and we won 92 games."

Said Grieve: "We told Orlando, 'If you take him, you have to play him. He can't sit on the bench.'

Orlando said, 'I'll play him.' And Pudge turned out to be one of the top prospects in that league. He was a high school senior age-wise, and he was more than holding his own in A ball."

Although players in the league were as much as five years older than Ivan was, he was a standout. In 112 games, he batted .238 with seven home runs, 42 RBIs and 22 doubles. Displaying his defensive skills came easier. He threw out 44 of 133 base-stealers (a 33 percent average—30 percent is considered good), and led the league's catchers in assists. Ivan also guided a pitching staff that included future major-leaguers Darren Oliver and Robb Nen to a division title. And as he would continue to do throughout his career, Ivan showed a willingness to learn and get better.

"I remember one game when there was a wild pitch, and he didn't run to get it quickly enough, so the runner went from first base to third," Gomez said. "So the next day, I had him out early, and we worked on blocking balls and other things. He challenged me. He said, 'I'm ready to go. I want to get better. Let's go.' I could tell from his first game, by the way he was behind the plate and the way he swung the bat. I said, 'This kid is for real.'"

Off the field, Ivan struggled to learn English and adapt to his new surroundings. When he first arrived in Florida in the spring of 1989, he didn't even know the word *yes*. He would phone Puerto

Rico often to speak to his parents, and to Maribel, who had lived for 14 years in New York City before moving to Puerto Rico, and through the years has helped Ivan improve his English.

"If I had to go to Puerto Rico and play baseball when I was 17, I would have been done in a hurry," Grieve said. "I would have been calling my parents to bring me back home. I had a tough time adjusting to playing winter ball in Venezuela, and I was 23 or 24 when I was there."

Ivan also leaned heavily on the assistance of Gomez and his wife, Nylsa. Whether it was cooking rice and beans, doing laundry or taking him shopping, Nylsa helped Ivan adapt, and even taught English to Ivan and some of the Rangers' other Latin minor-leaguers. Ivan remains grateful for the Gomez's influence and guidance that season.

"Orlando and his wife helped me a lot in Gastonia," Ivan said. "They took care of me like a son. I was still single, in a strange country, and didn't speak much English at the time. I owe them a lot. They mean a lot to me."

Said Gomez: "We still talk a lot now. If he sees my wife in the stands, he'll blow kisses to her. He was almost like a kid in the family."

Another Rangers coach had a big influence on Ivan. During that first spring training, Chino Cadahia was the one who gave Ivan the nickname Pudge, which now is used as much or more than

Ivan's given first name. At the time, Ivan was five-nine and a stocky 180 pounds, and didn't particularly like the nickname. But he grew to accept it on his quick path to the major leagues.

"From the day Ivan started playing, all of our coaches and scouts said, 'He could catch in the big leagues right now,'" Grieve said. "Even when he was 17, playing for Orlando in Gastonia. The question was how much was he going to hit."

For the 1990 season, Ivan was assigned to Class A Port Charlotte, Florida, where the Rangers also have their spring-training complex. Even with the step up into the tougher Florida State League, Ivan improved to a 39 percent success rate in throwing out base-stealers, which led the league. That pattern of improvement in each season would be one Ivan would continue throughout his career, even long after he reached the major leagues.

"I keep working," Ivan said. "I try to learn things every day. I want to improve and become a better player. You have to keep working hard, and try to do everything you can to get better."

Ivan was named the Florida State League's all-star catcher, and led the league's catchers with 727 putouts and 842 chances. He also improved his batting average up to .287, which was 15th best in the league, and led the team with 55 RBIs. Ivan's potential was noticed by *Baseball America* magazine, which named him the best defensive catcher in the

Florida State League, as well as the league's best major-league prospect overall.

At the time, Rangers farm director Marty Scott said Ivan was the first player he had seen who could make the jump from Class A to the major leagues. That might have happened in the Rangers' 1991 spring-training camp, but a hand injury kept Ivan from doing so. But it was only a matter of months before Ivan would be in the big leagues to stay at age 19.

The 1991 Rangers had a collection of veteran catchers, but none who fit the bill as an everyday player. Geno Petralli, John Russell and Mike Stanley were the trio that manager Bobby Valentine mixed and matched. In spring training, Ivan clearly was the superior thrower of the bunch, but his offense and maturity level were still in question. Once he was injured, Ivan was ticketed to start the season at Class AA Tulsa. It didn't take him long to prove he was too good for that level.

At Tulsa, Ivan threw out an incredible 23 of 39 base-stealers over the first two months of the season, and he did it despite missing some time with a sore arm in May. This prompted manager Bobby Jones to tell a reporter, "He's head and shoulders above everybody else. It's my 25th year in pro ball, and I've never seen anybody his age ready to step right into the big leagues. It's scary sometimes. It's unbelievable how hard this kid wants to work. Some kids you have to push. But this one comes up begging for it. His attitude and work ethic are outstanding."

Offensively, Ivan still needed to develop. He batted .274 with three home runs and 29 RBIs in the first 50 games. Five of those RBIs came on May 30 against San Antonio. He remained too impatient at the plate, walking only six times in 175 at-bats. But the call came, and on the fateful day of June 20, 1991, Ivan—all of 19 years, six months and 20 days old—was in the majors to stay, leaving a void at Tulsa that Jones knew wouldn't be filled.

"I thought I was ready for the big leagues," Ivan said. "I went there to try to do the same things I had done in the minors."

Said Jones: "We can't replace him, no matter whom they bring here."

Sure enough, despite playing only 50 games with Tulsa, Ivan was named to the Texas League's All-Star team at the end of the season. By that time, he had gone on to bigger and better things; he already was the talk of the American League.

CHAPTER FOUR
Making an Impression

After his impressive debut in Chicago, there was no getting Ivan out of the lineup. He wasn't the youngest player ever to wear a Rangers uniform. That distinction belongs to pitcher David Clyde, who was 18 years and two months old when he made his debut in 1973, followed by Wilson Alvarez, who was 19 and four months when he made one start in 1989 before returning to the minors. But Ivan was by far the most successful.

In the hours that followed his major-league debut, all Ivan could worry about was the next game. That was when he would fulfill a dream by being the starting catcher for the great Nolan Ryan, the Rangers' right-hander who would go into the Baseball Hall of Fame in 1999. Ivan became the first teenager to catch for a pitcher who was at least 40 years old (Ryan was 44) since 1963. Only 27 teenagers in major-league history have played more games in a season.

Ivan started 81 of the Rangers' final 102 games that season, and caught 88 in all—the second-most in major-league history by a teenager, trailing only Frankie Hayes' total of 89 games caught for the Philadelphia A's in 1934. The last

19-year-old to catch as many as 63 games was Del Crandall of the Boston Braves in 1949.

Ivan's hitting was far better than expected, as he batted .422 (19 for 45) in his first 12 games, and .362 (25 for 69) in his first 19 games. He had four hits against Oakland on July 2, and batted .333 with runners in scoring position for the year. His average was as high as .301 through August 11 before falling over the final six weeks. Ivan hit his first home run on August 30 off Kansas City's Storm Davis, making him the youngest player in Rangers' history to do so. He hit two more in a six-game span and finished with three homers and 27 RBIs, and a .264 batting average in 280 at-bats. The .264 average was tied for second among American League rookies with 250 or more at-bats, trailing only Minnesota's Chuck Knoblauch (.281), and that was despite Ivan's walking only five times.

"Nobody who comes up to the majors from Double A at age 19 hits great, except maybe Ken Griffey, Jr.," Grieve said. "But Ivan made great contact, so you could see he would be a great hitter with experience. He held his own that first year."

But it was on the strength of his arm and overall defensive play that Ivan was a unanimous choice as the Rangers' Rookie of the Year, and a fourth-place finisher in the American League Rookie of the Year balloting behind Knoblauch, Toronto's Juan Guzman and Detroit's Milt Cuyler.

Ivan threw out 34 of 70 base-stealers for the best percentage (48.6) among regular American League catchers, and second best in the majors behind Montreal's Gilberto Reyes (50.6). He threw out two runners in a game on seven different occasions, and caught 10 of 13 runners between August 30 and September 10. Ivan's 48.6 percentage that year is the seventh-best recorded by any catcher since 1989, and he also holds four of the other top six figures: 52.5 percent in 1998, 51.9 percent in 1997, 49 percent in 1992, and 48.9 percent in 1996. Only Reyes and Ron Karkovice of the Chicago White Sox (50 percent in 1993) were able to crack Ivan's domination.

Ivan also made a habit of picking off runners from first and second base with surprisingly quick throws. He picked runners off in successive games July 21 and 22, but runners not running out of fear of Ivan's arm were just as impressive.

"The guy who isn't a base-stealer, but used to steal against us, never runs against us any more," Valentine said at the time. "They'll hit and run with a guy like that, but they'll never try a straight steal. And the good base-stealer has to get a good jump to steal on us. It was easy for Ivan to impress, and he liked to. You know, if you got it, flaunt it. Infield practice was a fun thing to watch."

Added Grieve: "I don't know how you could say anybody throws better. Not with the way he picks runners off base. Maybe Bench was equal, but if there was someone better than Pudge, I couldn't tell you who it was."

And it wasn't just the Rangers' coaches who were singing Ivan's praises. California Angels manager Buck Rodgers, a former major-league catcher, said that Ivan, "could be the best we'll see."

For all his rookie success, Ivan only wanted to improve. He returned to Puerto Rico and played winter ball briefly for Mayaguez. He also undertook a weightlifting and conditioning program that reshaped his body, adding 10 pounds of muscle by the following spring, bringing him to 205 pounds. His goals for the 1992 season—his first full season in the majors—were lofty:"I

Ivan's hard work and dedication led to his steady improvement and development into one of the game's top hitting catchers.

want to hit .300 and play in the All-Star Game and win a Gold Glove Award. I want to do it this year. I don't want to wait."

As the youngest player in the majors for the second consecutive season, Ivan made good on two-thirds of his goals. Once again, he threw out the highest percentage of base-stealers in the American League, catching 51 of 104 for 49 percent. No other catcher threw out more than 44 percent. Ivan also became the third youngest player to receive a Gold Glove Award, which goes to the best defensive player at each position. Only second baseman Ken Hubbs of the Chicago Cubs in 1962 and Bench for the 1968 Cincinnati Reds were younger when they won Gold Gloves. Ivan, at 20 years and seven months, also became the fourth-youngest position player and eighth-youngest player to appear in the All-Star Game.

Said teammate Julio Franco during that season: "He can be as good as he wants to be. If he wants to be a star, he'll be a star. If he wants to be a superstar, he'll be a superstar. He's got everything it takes."

Through the first 34 games of the 1992 season, Ivan threw out 15 of 25 base-stealers, including the best in the American League at the time. In an April series in Arlington, Texas, against the Oakland A's, Ivan gunned down baseball's all-time leading base-stealer Rickey Henderson. The next day,

Henderson remained anchored at first base, not testing Ivan again.

Ivan also threw out Pat Listach twice in a game on May 10. Listach would go on to finish behind Henderson with 54 steals. That was one of seven times Ivan threw out two runners in a game. And on July 21 at Milwaukee and August 31 at Kansas City, Ivan caught three base-stealers. He also picked off five runners, and won the Gold Glove despite being charged with 15 errors, 10 on throws. Ivan's 116 games behind the plate were the fourth most in major-league history for a catcher aged 20 or under, and made him the only catcher in major-league history to lead his team in games caught at both age 19 and 20.

"I didn't think I could win a Gold Glove Award so early, but I'm happy to take it," Ivan said. "I don't want to stop here. I want to keep getting better and win the Gold Glove every year."

Rockies broadcaster Jim Sundberg, who won six Gold Glove Awards of his own as a catcher for the Rangers, added: "At this point, he easily is one of the most talented for his age I've ever seen."

Ivan fell far short of .300, finishing at .260 with eight homers and 37 RBIs in 420 at-bats. But that mark was the third highest among American League catchers who played in at least 100 games. He hit .324 in the first 23 games, but fell to .280 by June 6, when he went onto the disabled list for three weeks with a slight stress fracture in his lower back, as well as a thumb injury. One day earlier, Ivan and Maribel's first child, Ivan Dereck, had been born.

Ivan got hot when he came off the disabled list, going 11 for 30 to raise his average to .294 just before the All-Star break. That was enough to get him on the American League squad as a reserve, and he went hitless in two at-bats in the game played at San Diego's Jack Murphy Stadium. But after the All-Star break, Ivan hit a prolonged slump. He did not hit a home run in his final 66 games, and had just three RBIs in the final 36 games. Although he

One of the many Gold Glove Awards that Ivan has received

was a bit more selective than in his rookie season, Ivan's free swinging cost him many at-bats.

"He chased the ball up in the strike zone too much," said Valentine, who was replaced as manager by Toby Harrah in the middle of the 1992 season. "He wasn't disciplined. But I liked his ability to hit the ball to right field. And he understood hitting. He wasn't fooled by the breaking ball. As a young kid, he could hit it, so I knew he eventually would be a .300 hitter."

Eventually would be three years away, but Ivan already had begun what would be a nearly unprecedented double streak of All-Star Game appearances and Gold Glove Awards that would span the rest of the decade.

CHAPTER FIVE
Reaching Superstar Status

When asked for a Spanish word that best described Ivan's relentless style of play, Luis Mayoral, who broadcasts Rangers games in Spanish, said *el guerrero*, or *the warrior*.

"He wears the tools of ignorance, which are like a shield," Mayoral said. "And just the way he plays the game—always to win. *El guerrero*, the great warrior. He's always in there playing hard. He's peppy all the time. He never surrenders."

Added Tom Grieve: "The thing he has that you can't teach is an amazing joy and enthusiasm about playing the game of baseball. It could be 100 degrees, he could have played 20 days in a row, and he'll come out on the field, fire the ball around and be talking and smiling."

By the 1993 season, many others saw the same things as Mayoral and Grieve. Ivan's energetic and exciting style of play, plus his unmatched throwing ability, had made him a favorite both in Texas and around the entire American League. For the first time, he was voted by the fans as the starting catcher on the American League All-Star team.

At age 21 and seven months, Ivan became the youngest catcher and the seventh-youngest player to start an All-Star Game, tied with Joe

DiMaggio, Frank Robinson and Al Kaline (who, like DiMaggio, are Hall of Famers), along with Ken Griffey, Jr., who almost certainly will be elected to the Hall of Fame someday, also are among that elite group. In the game, played in Baltimore's Camden Yards, Ivan played the first five innings, doubled for his first All-Star hit and scored a run in a 9-3 American League victory.

Ivan finished with the best season of his career, setting major-league highs for catchers in games caught (134), batting average (.273), at-bats (473), runs (56), hits (129), triples (four), home runs (10), RBIs (66) and stolen bases (eight). His 10 homers were the most by a Rangers' catcher since Don Slaught hit 13 in 1986, and his 66 RBIs were the most ever by a Rangers catcher.

Ivan also earned a second Gold Glove Award, as he had an errorless streak of 41 games, threw out 38.5 percent of base-stealers, and ranked second among American League catchers in assists (76), third in putouts (801) and total chances (885), and sixth in fielding percentage (.991). The only other player in major-league history who won two Gold Gloves at a younger age than Ivan was Johnny Bench, who was one week younger than Ivan was when he was awarded his second Gold Glove in 1969. The only other Rangers who have been awarded at least two Gold Gloves in succession were Sundberg and third baseman Buddy Bell.

Just as in 1992, Ivan's season was marked by ups and downs offensively. He hit .362 through May 2, and was at .325 on June 1. But an extended slump over the next 33 games dropped him to .260 on July 22. One week later, he suffered a fractured left cheekbone on a freak play, as he was struck by Hubie Brooks' backswing. Ivan had to undergo surgery the following day, but was back in the lineup three days later, although he still was suffering from dizziness.

Ivan went on another hot streak upon his return, hitting .391 over 27 games to raise his average to .291 on August 26, but batted only .204 over his final 29 games, as the suffocating heat of the summer in north Texas took its toll.

Ivan shows off one of his eight Gold Glove Awards for fielding excellence, with Hall-of-Fame catcher Johnny Bench and Kirt Manwaring.

That heat traditionally has had a negative affect on the Rangers in the second half of the season, and is one of the reasons the team went its first 25 years in Texas without so much as a post-season appearance. That wasn't the case in 1993, as, under new manager Kevin Kennedy, the Rangers played better in the second half than they did in the first. Still, that wasn't enough, as they finished 86-76 for a nine-game improvement over 1993 but good enough only for a second-place finish in the American League West division behind the Chicago White Sox.

The season also marked the farewell to two fixtures of the Rangers' franchise: Nolan Ryan, who retired after a Hall of Fame career that included a record 5,714 strikeouts and seven no-hitters, and Arlington Stadium, a minor-league park that had been built up over the years to just bring it up to big-league standards. There would be no replacing Ryan, but the team would move into the stunning new Ballpark in Arlington for the 1994 season.

The Ballpark opened on April 11 to a sellout crowd of 46,056 fans, a record crowd in Arlington, but the Rangers couldn't pull out a victory in their debut game in their new home, losing 4-3 to the Milwaukee Brewers. It was the beginning of an odd season that would end prematurely on August 12, when the players went on strike due to a dispute with team owners.

The Rangers found themselves in first place in the American League West at the time of the strike, but there would be no post-season play that year. And even though they were in first place, it was more by process of elimination than anything else, as their record was a disappointing 52-62. Amazingly, they had moved into first place for good on May 30 with a win at Milwaukee that put their record at 22-26, and stayed there until the strike.

Ivan's season again was one of improvement over the previous year. In fact, in all but one of his major-league seasons, he has had a better batting average than the year before. This time, he fell just short of the .300 mark, hitting .298. He also set a career high with 16 homers despite the shortened season.

But the season also was marked by a series of injuries for Ivan, beginning with tendinitis in his right knee that first struck while he was playing winter ball in Puerto Rico. He played only two weeks in Puerto Rico before stopping because of the injury, and then spent the rest of the winter in a rehabilitation program.

The knee problem recurred during the Rangers' season, but Ivan played in 99 of the team's 114 games, missing two games in April after being hit on the elbow by a pitch, four more in May because of a strained right groin, and three more in June because of a jammed right thumb.

But none of those injuries stopped Ivan from making the All-Star team for the third consecutive season or from winning his third consecutive Gold Glove Award. Once again, he was voted in by fans as the American League's starting catcher. This time he played the entire 10-inning game in Pittsburgh's Three Rivers Stadium, and had his best All-Star game to date with two singles and one run scored in five at-bats in the American League's 8-7 loss. Only four other catchers had caught more than nine innings in an All-Star Game, and nobody since Bench in 1975 had caught an entire All-Star Game. Of course, Ivan was the youngest to do so.

The Gold Glove came his way after he threw out 19 of 56 base-stealers for the second-best percentage in the American League behind Oakland's Terry Steinbach. Ivan also led American League catchers with 96 starts, and had his then-career-best fielding percentage of .992.

For the first time, Ivan also won a Silver Slugger Award, which goes to the best offensive performer at each position. No American League catcher hit higher than Ivan's .298 mark, which also set a club record for Rangers' catchers.

Ivan was hitting only .230 through 17 games, but batted .311 in his last 82 and just missed hitting .300 for the first time. His hottest stretch came when he drove in 13 runs in a nine-game span from

July 9 to 20, and he also had a nine-game hitting streak from June 9 to 18.

But it all came to a premature end on August 12, leaving baseball-crazy Ivan without the game he loves.

It was late April when the 1995 season began, and meanwhile Kennedy had been replaced as manager by Johnny Oates, the fourth manager in Ivan's first five major-league seasons. Ivan kept as busy as possible during the streak, playing for Caguas in the Puerto Rican winter league, and for the Puerto Rican team that reached the Caribbean World Series.

The late start to the season proved to be worth the wait, as it was a memorable one for him on and off the field. On June 21, Maribel delivered the couple's second child, Amanda Christine. And Ivan added some new accomplishments to what was becoming his annual combination of a Gold Glove Award and All-Star Game appearance. This time, he was the Rangers' player of the year for leading the team in batting average (.303), total bases (221) and doubles (32), and setting a club record for RBIs by a catcher with 67. No catcher ever had led the Rangers in batting average. Ivan also won his second Silver Slugger Award, joining Parrish as the only American League catchers to win both a Silver Slugger and Gold Glove in two seasons.

The All-Star Game was a special moment. Besides being the fourth American League catcher to start three consecutive All-Star Games, this time Ivan got to play in front of his hometown fans at The Ballpark in Arlington. The game was played in 100-degree heat, and Ivan played the first five innings, going hitless in three at-bats.

"I'll never forget the ovation I got from the fans," Ivan said. "That is something I'll always remember. It was great to get to play the game in front of our fans."

In winning his fourth Gold Glove Award, Ivan led the majors by throwing out 43.7 percent of base-stealers, and was first in the American league

Ivan saves a run by applying a tag on New York's Wade Boggs to get an out at home plate.

in assists. He also picked off six runners, and threw out four more trying to advance on wild pitches.

It was also during the 1995 season that Ivan started a charitable foundation that aids underprivileged children, especially those battling cancer. To one of those children, he had an extra-special gift—another one of those too-good-to-be-true moments in Ivan's career. During the last game of the season, team president Tom Schieffer had Ivan meet five-year-old muscular dystrophy victim Matthew Swinton. Before an at-bat, Ivan had the boy kiss his bat for good luck. And on the first pitch he saw, Ivan hit a home run. He circled the bases clapping and pointing at the boy. Then after he crossed home plate, Ivan went over to Matthew, hugged him and gave him a high five.

"It was like something out of a movie," Ivan said. "I asked the kid, 'Is there good luck in that kiss?' He nodded yes. Then I hit the first pitch for a home run. That gave me immense satisfaction."

Said Schieffer: "I get the feeling that Babe Ruth was up there somewhere and smiling."

CHAPTER SIX
To the Playoffs

To know the history of the Texas Rangers is to know failure and futility. Born in 1961 as the second Senators franchise in Washington, D.C., the team lost 100 or more games in its first four seasons, and finished in last place in three of its first four seasons. The best the Senators could do in the decade of the 1960s was a fourth-place finish in 1969.

For the 1972 season, owner Bob Short moved the financially troubled franchise to the Dallas-Fort Worth area, and renamed it the Rangers. But other than a second-place finish in 1974 and a third-place finish in 1978, things didn't improve much. There were a handful of winning seasons, but no division titles. In fact, the Rangers rarely played a meaningful game in September because they usually were too far out of the pennant race. And when the Rangers were at their best in the late-1980s, they were overshadowed by the Oakland A's dynasty, so the best they could do was second place. The trials and tribulations were so ingrained in the franchise that a book about it, entitled *The Impossible Takes a Little Longer*, was published in 1990.

But things would be different in 1996. The Rangers stayed in first place in the American League

West division for all but three days in April, clinched their first-ever division title on September 27, and won the division by four and a half games.

With the team's success came individual honors. Juan Gonzalez was named the American League's Most Valuable Player after hitting .314 with 47 home runs and 144 RBIs. Oates was named American League Co-Manager of the Year, and Ivan added another Gold Glove Award and Silver Slugger Award, made another All-Star Game start, and put himself in the major-league record book with a few more accomplishments. In the All-Star Game in Philadelphia, he went hitless in two at-bats, but showed off his powerful arm by throwing out both Barry Bonds and Lance Johnson on the bases.

The New York Yankees were the Rangers' first-round playoff opponent, and Gonzalez—just as he had done throughout the regular season—carried the Rangers against them. Texas won the first game, 6-2, in Yankee Stadium, as Gonzalez, who went 7 for 16 with five home runs and nine RBIs in four games, hit a three-run homer off David Cone in a five-run fourth inning.

The Rangers let a 4-1 lead slip away in Game 2, and eventually lost 5-4 in 12 innings in a game that turned around the series. Gonzalez hit two more homers and drove in all four runs, but the Rangers didn't score after the fourth inning.

Ivan got his second hit of the series in Game 3, an RBI double that put the Rangers ahead 2-1 in the fifth. It stayed that way until the ninth, when Darren Oliver gave up back-to-back singles, and then Mike Henneman gave up a sacrifice fly and an RBI single for a 3-2 Yankees win.

In the final game, Texas built a 4-0 lead. But eight different Rangers pitchers couldn't keep the Yankees from a comeback, and Cecil Fielder's RBI single in the seventh put eventual World Champion New York Yankees ahead for good, 6-4.

Ivan got three hits in the final game to finish the series 6 for 16 (.375) with two RBIs. But take away Gonzalez's great series, and the rest of the Rangers batted only .190 with one homer and seven RBIs.

One of Ivan's six hits was a double, giving him 48 for the season. He hit 44 of those while playing catcher in the regular season, giving him the major-league record for doubles, two more than Detroit's Mickey Cochrane (1930), San Diego's Terry Kennedy (1982) and Minnesota's Brian Harper (1990).

Ivan's total of 639 at-bats also was a major-league record for catchers, breaking Bench's mark of 621 set in 1974. Two things worked in Ivan's favor in this case. He usually batted second in the Rangers' order, higher than most catchers, who are usually slow runners, and his free-swinging that leads to few walks.

Ivan just missed two more major-league records for catchers, as his 192 hits were just one short of the record held by Joe Torre (1964) and Ted Simmons (1975), and his 116 runs were just two short of Cochrane's 1932 total.

Climbing further up the Gold Glove Award charts with his fifth in a row, Ivan tied Bill Freehan for fourth place among catchers. The only ones who stood ahead of him were Sundberg and Bob Boone,

Chasing a foul pop fly, Ivan goes head over heels near the third base dugout at The Ballpark in Arlington.

who won seven in the 1970s and 1980s, and Bench, who won 10 in a row from 1968 to 1977. When interviewed in his home that winter, Ivan said there were spots reserved in his trophy case for 14 Gold Glove Awards, the number he has in mind to win in his career. It is that kind of confidence, dedication and determination that kept earning him praise from managers, coaches and players around the game.

Said teammate Rafael Palmeiro: "His arm is a gift, but he's worked hard at it. He's really worked hard to round out his whole game. Now, he's stealing bases. His hitting gets better every year. He wants to stay the best. He amazes me every day."

Added Grieve: "Nobody knows how hard he works. He and Juan both. If you sit in the lobby on the road, you'll see them every morning at 9:30-10:00, going to work out with a personal trainer. They work out a couple hours every day. They're in as good a shape as you can be. They know what it takes to make the Hall of Fame, in terms of numbers and commitment. They're willing to pay the price."

Phillies catcher Mike Lieberthal said he tries to spend time talking to Ivan each spring. "I try to get as much out of him as I can. He's definitely one guy I watch more than any other. He's one of the few catchers who play 150 games a year. That's something I want to do."

The 1997 season reached late July with the Rangers in the midst of an injury-filled and disappointing season. By the time the year was over, a total of 14 different players spent 18 stints on the disabled list, combining to miss 642 games. None of those injuries was bigger than the torn ligament in Gonzalez's left thumb that cost him 31 days of the season. Pitcher Roger Pavlik also missed most of the season after undergoing elbow surgery, and key players Will Clark, John Burkett, Ken Hill, Mark McLemore, and Mickey Tettleton also were idled for long stretches.

But potentially worse news cropped up in July. Ivan was in his final year before he would become eligible for free agency, and contract talks between his agent and the Rangers hadn't produced a deal. There even was speculation that the Rangers would do the unthinkable and trade Ivan before the July 31 trading deadline, prompted by their inability to reach a contract agreement. On July 29, the Rangers protected themselves from the possible loss of Ivan by trading for veteran catcher Jim Leyritz.

Ivan also was troubled by the contract dispute. The most the Rangers had offered was five years and $38 million, and his agent had asked for about $7 million more. Ivan talked to Gonzalez, his longtime friend, and also to his mother. And on the morning of July 31, on an off day following a road trip, he took matters into his own hands.

Without his agent's knowledge, Ivan paid a visit to Schieffer's office. It wasn't long before a deal was reached. Ivan didn't want to play anyplace else, and told Schieffer so. Touched by Ivan's sincerity, Schieffer increased the club's offer, and by that afternoon, Ivan agreed to a five-year deal worth $42 million. Undoubtedly, he could have received as much as $10-20 million more if he had become a free agent and signed with another team, but Ivan wanted to stay with the Rangers, the team he called "my family."

The season may have been a lost cause, as the Rangers finished 77-85 and in third place in the American League West, but at least Ivan knew where he would be through the 2002 season—and that's exactly the way he and the Rangers wanted it.

Ivan finished the 1997 season with a few more career bests and first-time accomplishments, along with his sixth consecutive Gold Glove Award and fourth consecutive Silver Slugger Award. No American League catcher had won the latter honor four years in a row, and only Sundberg won as many as six Gold Glove Awards in the American League. Ivan also established a new career high with a .313 batting average, and a new career high with 20 home runs, the most ever by a Rangers catcher. Three of those home runs came in the same game against Minnesota on September 11, marking only the eighth time an American League catcher had hit three homers in a game. The .313 batting average was the highest by any American League catcher since Carlton Fisk's .315 mark in 1977.

And for the third consecutive season, and the fifth time in his seven years, Ivan lead the majors in throwing out base-stealers, catching 40 of 77 (or 51.7%), the first time he had been above the 50-percent mark in the big leagues. But as good of a year as Ivan enjoyed, he was about to take his career to another level.

CHAPTER SEVEN
Hall of Fame Material

T he 1998 season was almost a repeat of 1996, and that was a good thing for Ivan and the Rangers.

At least until the playoffs. The Rangers again won the American League West division title, this time with an 88-74 record, the third-best record in club history. Gonzalez also won the American League Most Valuable Player Award again, becoming only the 12th player in American League history to win more than one and joining Hall of Famers such as Yogi Berra, Joe DiMaggio, Jimmie Foxx, Hank Greenberg, Mickey Mantle, Ted Williams, and Robin Yount.

Ivan's lock on the catchers' Gold Glove Award continued; his seventh in a row was the most in American League history, and tied him for the second-most in major-league history with Boone, trailing only Bench. His .321 average was eighth best in the league and ninth highest in Rangers history. It also was his fourth consecutive .300 or better season, tying Al Oliver for the Rangers' record.

Ivan also established three new career highs, hitting 21 homers, driving in 91 runs and stealing nine bases, which led to his fifth consecutive Silver Slugger Award, third most by a catcher in major-league history. By stealing nine bases without being caught, he tied a Rangers' record. The newfound speed was in part credited to Ivan's continued hard work in the off-season to improve all facets of his game. His personal trainer, Edgar Diaz, who has competed as a pole vaulter in two Olympic Games for Puerto Rico, emphasized stretching, flexibility, and speed in Ivan's training program.

Ivan has been an American League All-Star every year since 1992.

There was another appearance in the All-Star Game, his seventh in a row and sixth consecutive start. This one came at Coors Field in Denver, where he enjoyed his best All-Star Game, getting three singles, driving in a run, scoring a run and stealing a base. No other catcher in All-Star history had hit three singles in a game. That brought his All-Star Game batting average to .300, 6 for 20.

And for the sixth time in eight years, including the last four in succession, Ivan led the majors by throwing out 42 of 80 base-stealers, for his career-best percentage of 52.5 percent. All that was left was for him to take his team to the playoffs.

Unfortunately, the Rangers found themselves matched once again with the New York Yankees, who were coming off one of the greatest regular seasons in history, one in which they won an amazing 114 games. And the Yankees would win the first three games of the best-of-five series with the Rangers for a sweep on their way to their second World Series championship in three years.

The Rangers didn't have to search hard for reasons for their downfall, as the team hit just .141 (13 for 92) in the three games, and scored only one run on their way to losing 2-0, 3-1 and 4-0. Yankees pitchers David Wells and Mariano Rivera limited Texas to five hits in the first game (nobody had more than one). Andy Pettitte, Jeff Nelson and Rivera allowed only five in game two, when Ivan drove in the only Rangers' run with a fifth-inning single that scored Gonzalez. And in game three, home runs by Paul O'Neill and Shane Spencer were more than enough, as David Cone and three relievers gave up only three hits, including two by third baseman Todd Zeile. Even Gonzalez, who was so potent in the 1996 series, was silenced, as he went 1 for 12. Ivan's only hit in 10 at-bats was the RBI single in game two.

"It was exciting to be in the playoffs both times," Ivan said. "Getting that close and maybe being able to play in a World Series is what every player wants to do. I liked the atmosphere in New York and in Texas. It was exciting. It's a great feeling to go into the playoffs. Too bad we lost both series."

Ivan's off-season work with Diaz really paid off in the 1999 season. That, plus not playing winter ball for the first time, left Ivan faster and fresher for his ninth major-league season at age 27. The latter idea came from Johnny Oates, who saw Ivan wearing down late in each season due to his heavy workload (Ivan entered the 1999 season having caught 81.6 percent of all Rangers games since he entered the majors).

With more stolen bases as one of his goals for the season, Ivan not only set a career high, he added another record to his growing list of accomplishments by becoming the first catcher in major-league history to hit at least 20 bases and steal at least 20 bases. In fact, Ivan accomplished the feat by August 14 in Chicago, when he stole his 20th base to go with 24 homers at the time. The closest any other catcher had come to 20 homers and 20 steals was when Benito Santiago hit 18 homers and stole 21 bases in 1987. Only two other catchers in American League history stole more than 20

In his best season to date—1999—Ivan set an American League record for home runs by a catcher with 35. He also stole 25 bases to become the first catcher in major league history to hit at least 20 homers and steal at least 20 bases.

bases—Kansas City's John Wathan (36 in 1982 and 28 in 1983), and Chicago's Ray Schalk (30 in 1916 and 24 in 1914).

"I credit my personal trainer, Edgar Diaz, for my success in stealing bases the past couple of years," Ivan said.

In June, when Ivan actually had more stolen bases of his own than those allowed to opponents, Colorado manager Jim Leyland paid him the ultimate compliment. He said his team wouldn't be trying to steal against Ivan. "When you talk about the best player in the game, his name has to be up there, doesn't it?"

Leyland said before the start of a series between his Rockies and the Rangers. "He's got 15 stolen bases, and he's only allowed nine. He dominates his position, offensively and defensively. That's what a great player does. He's not going to throw anybody out tonight. He can rest his arm. He may pick somebody off, but he's not going to throw anybody out stealing."

Ivan finished the season with 25 stolen bases, and smashed his previous career highs in several other categories. He batted .332 to raise his career batting average above .300 for the first time to .307, belted 35 homers (14 more than he had hit in any other season), knocked in 113 runs (22 more than his previous best), fell one hit short of 200 with 199, and tied his career high with 116 runs scored.

The Rangers again won the American League West by a comfortable margin over the Oakland Athletics, but once again ran into the Yankees in the playoffs and quickly were eliminated in three games. Ivan had three hits in 12 at-bats, but couldn't help the usually powerful offense get going in the

For the first time in his major-league career, Ivan became a solid candidate to win the American League MVP Award in 1999.

Besides his talent and his dedication to improve, Ivan always brings an enjoyment for the game to the ballpark.

playoffs. Texas scored only one run in the entire series.

As the Rangers moved into first place and held it for most of the season, Ivan's great individual season prompted Oates to start campaigning for him as the American League's Most Valuable Player.

"For me, with all due respect to the other guys, I've seen him every day and I know how valuable he is," Oates said. "I can be prejudiced, but it would be tough for me to vote for any other guy. I think Rafael Palmeiro's numbers are deserving, but when you look at Pudge's offense, what he's done for our ball club with the way he shuts down other team's running games, playing every day, the possibility he could have 100 runs and 100 RBIs, I think he is deserving.

"If he stays healthy, I guarantee he'll be making an acceptance speech [for the Hall of Fame] someday. In my 30 years in baseball, the closest total package I've seen to Pudge is Johnny Bench."

Ivan, who hit three homers in an April game against Seattle, and was on his way to throwing out more than 50 percent of base-stealers once again, downplayed his individual accomplishments.

"The MVP would be nice; it would be great," Ivan said. "But I'm trying not to think about it. I just need to keep doing what I'm doing. People say I'm the best, but that's for others to judge. I just go to the ballpark every day, and do the best job I can."

With Ivan and Palmeiro leading the way, the Rangers enjoyed their best-ever regular season, winning 95 games, one more than the 1977 team. That was good enough to give the Rangers their fourth American League West title in six years, and their second in a row. Included in the 95 wins was a 51-30 record at The Ballpark in Arlington. Only three other teams had more home wins.

But the 95 wins only earned the Rangers another matchup with the post-season nemesis, the New York Yankees, who lead the American League with a 98-64 record. And this series was almost an exact duplicate of the other two, as the Rangers were swept in the first three games of the best-of-five series, and once again couldn't muster any offense against the excellent Yankees pitching staff.

The tone for the series was set in Game 1, when the Yankees broke open a close game with a four-run sixth inning on their way to an 8-0 shut-out. Yankees starting pitcher Orlando Hernandez allowed only two hits and six walks over eight innings, and then Jeff Nelson completed the shutout. The big hits were provided by Yankees center fielder Bernie Williams, who collected six RBIs on a two-run double in the fifth inning, and a three-run homer in the sixth inning, and a run-scoring single in the eighth inning. Ivan got both of the Rangers' hits (a double and a single) and also stole a base. But the rest of the lineup combined to go hitless in 23 at-bats against Hernandez and Nelson.

Game 2 was much closer, but again the Yankees prevailed, 3-1, breaking a tie with a run in the seventh and adding another in the eighth. Yankees starting pitcher Andy Pettitte allowed a solo home run to Gonzalez in the fourth but little else, and Nelson and Mariano Rivera finished with 1 2/3 hitless innings.

Ivan had one hit in four at-bats, as Texas totaled only seven hits.

Not even The Ballpark in Arlington could help the Rangers, as the series moved there for Game 3. Once again, they were shut out, 3-0, and got only five hits (all singles) — off Roger Clemens, Nelson and Rivera. After scoring 5.83 runs per game over the162-game regular season, the Rangers scored only one in the three-game series, and had a team batting average of just .152. That made it nine

Ivan and his Texas Rangers teammates haven't been able to get over the hump when it comes to post-season play. In the late 1990s, they lost in the first round of the playoffs to the New York Yankees in three of four years.

straight losses to the Yankees over three playoff series.

"I cannot explain what happened," a disappointed Palmeiro said. "I'll think about it all winter, and maybe I'll tell you why in spring training. Right now, it's kind of hard to believe."

Added shortstop Royce Clayton: "There are certain teams throughout history in all sports that have a nemesis. They happen to be ours."

Ivan finished the series with three hits in 12 at-bats, dropping his career post-season batting average to .263. But that was only a minor flaw in what had been one of the greatest seasons ever put together by a major-league catcher. Along the way, Ivan accomplished the following:

His 35 home runs were the most ever by an American League catcher, and 14 more than his previous high. He had five two-homer games, including his nine-RBI game on April 13 in Seattle, when he a hit three-run homer, his first career grand slam, and a two-run single. He also had back-to-back two homer games on August 15 and 16. In all, he hit 12 homers in the month of August, the most in any month by an active catcher.

His 25 stolen bases were the fifth highest in a season by a major-league catcher. Ivan swiped 15 bases in his first 51 games, including 11 in a row at one point. He also had two steals in a game on June

8. The combination of 35 homers and 25 steals made him the first catcher in major-league history to top 20 in both categories. His 113 RBIs were the most by an American League catcher since Detroit's Lance Parrish drove in 114 in 1983, and were tied for the second most by an American League catcher since 1957.

His nine-RBI game on April 13 in Seattle was the second-highest single-game total of the 1999 season, one behind Boston's Nomar Garciaparra, and made him only the third catcher ever to have as many as nine RBIs in a game, joining Walker Cooper and Smokey Burgess. Ivan also had a five-RBI game on June 25, and drove in four runs in a game three other times.

His 116 runs scored were the second-most in history by a major-league catcher, behind only Mickey Cochrane's 118 in 1932. It was only the 11th time a catcher had scored as many as 100 runs in a season, and was Ivan's second. Only Cochrane scored 100 runs more times than Ivan, with four.

With 116 runs and 113 RBIs, Ivan was only the eighth catcher in history to total at least 100 runs and RBIs in the same season.

Ivan threw out 39 of 72 would-be base-stealers for a 54.2 success rate, which led the majors for the fifth consecutive season, and was the highest percentage since that statistic started being kept in

1989. That brought his career success rate to 46.9 percent. He also picked off 10 runners to bring his total to 37 since the start of the 1996 season.

His .332 batting average was tied for the best by an American League catcher since New York's Bill Dickey hit .362 in 1936, and was the fifth highest in history by a catcher. It also marked his fifth consecutive season of .300 or better, and raised his career batting average to exactly .300, which would be the fourth highest in history by a catcher.

Ivan has led the majors in throwing out base-stealers in seven of his nine major league seasons.

In a tight contest, Ivan won the balloting by the Baseball Writers Association of America for the American League's Most Valuable Player. He was the first catcher honored since Thurman Munson of the New York Yankees in 1976.

It all was enough to make Orlando Gomez, who now was watching Ivan from the opposing dugout as a coach of the Tampa Bay Devil Rays, to shake his head in amazement at how far his former pupil had come.

"I saw he was going to be a good one," Gomez said. "But where he is now, I didn't see that. I thought he would be an above-average major-league player. But now he's a superstar. He's one of the best players in the game. If he keeps going, he could end up in the Hall of Fame. The biggest thing with him is that he loves what he's doing. You can see by the way he does things. He's proud of what he's doing."

No matter how successful Ivan becomes, he has never forgotten his roots. As soon as the baseball season ends, Ivan returns home to Puerto Rico. He no longer lives in the desperately poor barrio, Vega Baja, where he was born. But his father still lives there. Jose has refused his son's offers to move him to a better way of life somewhere else on the island. He continues to live in a cinder block house. Ivan comes back to visit all the people he has known since childhood. Every Tuesday night during the fall and winter, Ivan comes to Vega Baja to play a six-inning softball game with a group of locals.

Ivan, however, lives in an exclusive suburb of San Juan in a very expensive home, which he has owned since 1996. It is a half an hour's drive to Vega Baja. He lives here with his wife and children (son Dereck and daughter Amanda) in a huge house with Greek columns, white marble floors, crystal chandeliers, and a swimming pool. He loves a Sunday barbeque, listens to salsa music, plays video games for hours on end, and works out every day. He golfs, he swims, and has recently learned to scuba dive. He spends a lot of time at his house horsing around with his kids. Because he is away from home so much of the year, he cherishes every moment at home with his family.

Ivan's workout routine has made him into a very strong man. With only 11 percent body fat, his childhood nickname of "Pudge" is just a silly joke today. No matter what else Ivan is doing, baseball is never far from his mind. He is obsessed with the game. "It's easy to be lazy," he told Michael Geffner of *Sporting News.* "It is a long season. But I get paid a lot of money to play baseball and the fans want me to put on a show. So I'm always working to make myself better, to stay healthy, and to play every day... I want to improve everything in my game, to get better every year." Not yet out of his twenties, this superstar has many more years to shine.

CHRONOLOGY

1971   Born on November 30, in Vega Baja, Puerto Rico.

1988   Signs with the Texas Rangers on July 27.

1989   Makes professional debut in Gastonia, North Carolina.

1990   Marries Maribel Rivera and plays in first major-league game on June 20.

1992   Plays in first All-Star Game, in San Diego, and wins first Gold Glove Award.

1995   Is named Texas Rangers Player of the Year.

1996   Sets major-league record for doubles by a catcher.

1999   Sets major-league record by throwing out 54.7 percent of base-stealers. Becomes first major-league catcher to hit 20 homers and steal 20 bases, finishing the year with 35 and 25. Voted to the Associated Press Major League All Star team. Wins the American League Most Valuable Player in a tight contest.

MAJOR-LEAGUE STATISTICS

Year	Team	G	AB	R	H	2B	3B	HR	RBI	SB	.AVG
1991	Texas	88	280	24	74	16	0	3	27	0	.264
1992	Texas	123	420	39	109	16	1	8	37	0	.260
1993	Texas	137	473	56	129	28	4	10	66	8	.271
1994	Texas	99	363	56	108	19	1	16	57	6	.298
1995	Texas	130	492	56	149	32	2	12	67	0	.301
1996	Texas	153	639	116	192	47	3	19	86	5	.300
1997	Texas	150	597	98	187	34	4	20	77	7	.311
1998	Texas	145	579	88	186	40	4	21	91	9	.322
1999	Texas	144	600	116	199	29	1	35	113	25	.332
Totals		1169	4343	649	1333	261	20	144	621	60	.307

PLAYOFFS

Year	Team	G	AB	R	H	2B	3B	HR	RBI	SB	AVG
1996	Texas	4	16	1	6	1	0	0	2	0	.375
1998	Texas	3	10	0	1	0	0	0	1	0	.100
1999	Texas	3	12	0	3	1	0	0	0	1	.250
Totals		10	38	1	10	2	0	0	3	1	.263

ALL-STAR GAMES

Year	AB	R	H	2B	3B	HR	RBI	SB	AVG
1992	2	0	0	0	0	0	0	0	.000
1993	2	1	1	1	0	0	0	0	.500
1994	5	1	2	0	0	0	0	0	.400
1995	3	0	0	0	0	0	0	0	.000
1996	2	0	0	0	0	0	0	0	.000
1997	2	0	0	0	0	0	0	0	.000
1998	4	1	3	0	0	0	1	0	.000
1999	2	0	0	0	0	0	0	0	.000
Totals	22	3	6	1	0	0	1	0	.273

INDEX